Brontide

Brontide

Sue McPherson

Magabala
BOOKS

This is a 🐦 Magabala Book

LEADING PUBLISHER OF ABORIGINAL AND
TORRES STRAIT ISLANDER STORYTELLERS.
CHANGING THE WORLD, ONE STORY AT A TIME.

First published 2018, reprinted 2018, 2019 x2, 2020, 2021, 2022, 2023
Magabala Books Aboriginal Corporation
1 Bagot Street, Broome, Western Australia
Website: www.magabala.com   Email: sales@magabala.com

Magabala Books receives financial assistance from the Commonwealth Government
through the Australia Council, its arts advisory body. The State of Western
Australia has made an investment in this project through the Department of
Local Government, Sport and Cultural Industries. Magabala Books would like to
acknowledge the generous support of the Shire of Broome, Western Australia.

Magabala Books is Australia's only independent Aboriginal and Torres Strait
Islander publishing house. Magabala Books acknowledges the Traditional Owners
of the Country on which we live and work. We recognise the unbroken connection
to traditional lands, waters and cultures. Through what we publish, we honour all
our Elders, peoples and stories, past, present and future.

This manuscript won the State Library of Queensland's black&write! Indigenous
Writing Fellowship, a partnership between the black&write! Indigenous Writing
and Editing Project and Magabala Books.

Copyright © Sue McPherson, Text & Illustrations, 2018

The creator assert their moral rights.

Cover Design Jo Hunt
Typeset by Post Pre-press Group
Printed and bound by Griffin Press

978-1-925360-92-9 (Print)

A catalogue record for this
book is available from the
National Library of Australia

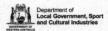

To Steve, Jardi boy and Jye Springall,
Pancho and Tony Ryan

Author's Note

G'day! My name is Sue and I'm the author of *Grace Beside Me*. Not that long ago I was asked to help with a storytelling workshop at Taralune High School.

Taralune is a quaint, old hippy beach town, halfway between Rainbow Beach and Noosa in mostly sunny Queensland. My plan was to recharge the battery, read, eat, enjoy the sunshine and help a few kids write a story. I honestly thought the trip was all about me and having time out ... I was wrong.

Taralune was fantastic – the school, the people and the sleepy beach culture were perfect for anyone needing a break. Workshops were held at two schools, Taralune High and St Nicholas Lutheran College.

We had a ball. Most of the kids enjoyed telling and writing a good yarn, especially a young lad named Pen. A few saw it as a bludge but put in anyway. And then there were Rob, Benny Boy and Jack who hated anything connected to reading or writing. They thought they had better things to do.

Those three lads didn't see themselves as storytellers but their doggedness to tell a yarn was both inspiring and profound.

The words, thoughts and images in these pages are theirs. I just asked questions, recorded and collated the information given to me.

I'm not trained in interviewing. Looking back now, my techniques were, at times, clunky, unconventional and embarrassing.

Like many, I felt the storm brewing but I didn't think it would hit. Many of us played hard growing up, but somehow we avoided tragedy. I assumed the same would happen in Taralune. My lack of intervention has caused me many sleepless nights. Should have, could have … but didn't. Writing this now, I can barely see the words as my tears well.

This is not my story, it's theirs. Stay strong, stay safe.

Everyone has a story.

Sue McPherson

Rob

Name:	Rob Bower
Age:	17
Year:	12
Pet:	Nig
Brothers:	Joey
	Pen (Kane)
Mum:	Shaz (Sharon)
Dad:	Dave – Pain in the Arse

Rob

Monday, 9am
Taralune High School, Library Room L4

Sue: Where do you want to start?

Rob: Miss, I don't want to do this.

        It's ucked.

Sue: Oi!

Rob: I didn't use the f.

Sue: We've talked about this. I can't transcribe
        swearing.

Rob: So, I can't swear?

Sue: Use your imagination.

Rob: I did. And anyway that sucks, 'cause I've got
        shitloads to say.

        Hey, Miss? I reckon the word shit's okay.

        Can I say shit? Because if I can't, well, then this
        isn't gonna work.

Sue: If you have to.

Rob: And I don't want no flappy ears listening.

Sue: It's a double room and we're at the back. Nobody can hear us.

Look around … See? They're all busy.

Rob: People think I'm always angry.

It pisses me off what they think. People piss me off. They think they know me, but they're full a shit.

I said shit and you said it's okay?

Sue: Keep going.

Rob: If I've got somethin' to say, I'll say it. I'm not like all those others-who-big-note all the time. Big mouths when they're all together but on their own quiet as mices.

Mouses.

Weak pricks, that's all they are. I'll stand up for meself. I'm definitely not weak so let's get that right. Okay?

Sue: Okay. Who are your mates?

Rob: There's Foot and Trev. I talk to them all the time,
        can't shut me up 'cause they're me mates, ya see.
        We got lots to talk about.

        And I've got Joey. Joey and Pen are me brothers
        so that doesn't count, does it?

Sue: Why not? If you have things in common and
        you get on?

Rob: Yeah … well, okay.

        Taralune is our hometown. Shaz's – Mum's –
        great-great-grandparents pulled up here years
        ago in a bullocky wagon after trying to scratch a
        living out west.

        If you look through the window, you'll see.

        This window, Miss … across them hills, it's
        blackfella country. Trev's mob comes from there
        too. Probably was his mob that worked for me
        great-great-grandparents.

Sue: Tell me about Trev? He's obviously a blackfella?

Rob: Yep, but he's not one of those lazy black bastards
        you see around.

Sue: Don't hold back.

Rob: I'm not. It's my story, remember?

But Trev's good. And his mum and his sister, they all wear shoes and they've got their own house. And Trev's mum is the best cook ever, even better than Shaz.

Sue: You say Aboriginal people are lazy black bastards?

Rob: Most are! So what?

Sue: So, it's derogatory. It's inappropriate. Not right.

What if I called you a lazy white bastard?

Rob: Sick shoes, Miss.

Sue: Tell me about your home.

Rob: Most houses here are Queenslanders, ours has been in our family since way back. Poppie added a few new rooms when he had it. Since him and Nan died we've painted all the rooms, dug a pool and built an entertainment area …

A new picket fence for the front and Shaz put

in a real cool garden. It's tropical but full of sick things like garden sculptures and seats and water features and shit.

Good shit, but!

Kids around here love it when we have an open garden.

Yeah, we also took down the shitter out the back, no need for a pit toilet these days, and we installed new fans and a wood heater inside.

Sue: How about your mum and dad?

Rob: When Dave came back the third time …

Dave's me dad.

Sue: Where did he go?

Rob: Dunno. He just pisses off and leaves us to it.

Anyway, when Dave came back he built a big shed out the back for his tools and trailers and bits of wood and stuff. He's a builder.

Joey, me brother, works for him and I'm a first-year apprentice even though I'm still at school.

6

School three days, two days at work. Except that's changed now, 'cause school's nearly finished.

Sue: Perfect! You've started your apprenticeship and in three weeks you'll have your school certificate as well.

Rob: Yeah! I have to complete Year Twelve and do an apprenticeship; Joey had to do the same.

If I did a different apprenticeship, Dave would have to change his signs to Dave Bower and Son, not Sons … and the ads in the paper and his Facebook page …

Dave said I'd be the dickhead if I changed me career.

Sue: What about Pen?

Rob: Pen's different. Dave said Pen won't be working with us.

Just me and Joey.

Sue: Why's Pen different?

Rob: Everyone knows he looks like Shaz.

Sue: I don't get it?

Rob: Don't worry, Miss, I'll tell ya later.

Sue: But it's your life, you boys should be able to choose your own career.

         Rob?

Rob: Not in our house ... having your own life isn't part of Dave's plan.

         We are his plan.

         So, the business is really takin' off. Dave's got eight blokes workin' for him, plus Joey and me. A new bloke started a couple of weeks ago, his name's Jack. He's my age, another apprentice, so, yeah, that means ten workers and the new bloke makes eleven.

Sue: Where's Jack from?

Rob: From here, this school. He come up from down south. Dave reckons he's a bit of a bogan sook.

         They're a different breed down south, that's what the old man says. I wouldn't know, I haven't been there, eh!

So, three more weeks and I'm finished with
Education Queensland.

Me and the boys will head down to the Goldie
for schoolies, go apeshit for a week then back
home and on the job as apprentice chippy.

Can't wait.

Sue: You don't like school?

Rob: Just because I'm doin' Year Twelve doesn't mean
I'm good at it, 'cause I suck.

I'm exceptional at maths, me report even says
that. I understand gardening, it's easy and fun.
Playing in dirt and looking after flowers and
trees and growin' things isn't work for me, I
actually enjoy it. And I'm good at it.

But I can't stand writing and thinking about
writing and people talking to me about writing.

I've never read a whole book in me life. But I've
watched all of Harry Potter.

I'm no good at all those other subjects. I'll get
passes but that's it.

I've already got a job so who the ...

9

P

H

U

K

cares?

Did you get that, Miss?

Sue: I got it.

Rob: Clever, eh? See! I'm being creative.

Sue: Tell me about girls, do you have a girlfriend?

Rob: Women?

         What can I say? I'm a chick magnet.

         Like, I'm not one of those stay-with-the-same-
         girl-for-twenty-years type of blokes. I'm more
         of a show-me-what-you've-got-and-how-often-
         can-you-give-it-to-me type.

Sue: You're killing me.

Rob: Well, women bore me. Leslie Peters, Mia Rose,
         Chrissie Lucas are all horny and hot as.

10

Good-lookin' but *booooorring*!

They always want the same thing.

Let's go to the movies.

Let's go out.

Let's hold hands.

Let's say we're in a relationship on Facebook.

Let's get jealous whenever another good-lookin' girl walks past.

Blah, blah, blah – they're all the same.

Sue: All?

Rob: Well …

Well, no …

Not Sharni Manning, Trev's sister …

She's different.

She's nice …

Sue: She's what?

Rob: You heard.

         Too bad she's …

         Well, it's too bad Dave doesn't see her as a good
         catch for his boys.

Sue: Sounds like a good bloke, your dad.

Rob: Miss, I'm not stupid, I know sarcasm.

Sue: She won't be Dave's girlfriend, she'll be yours.
         And I never said you were stupid.

Rob: I know that.

Sue: Tell me about your mum.

Rob: What abouta?

Sue: Well, who is she? What's she like?

Rob: Shaz loves music from the '70s and '80s. She
         listens to music a lot, just zones out and gets on
         with her work in the garden or in the house.

         She loves it here, the house is just about how she
         wants it, light and airy.

         A happy Queenslander living in a happy home.

Well, sometimes … it's happy when Dave goes on a fishin' trip or when there's work down the coast or in Brisbane or when he goes piggin' with his crusty old mates.

Yeah, it's happy then.

The block out at the Retreat has just been cleared. Dave hopes to start building the new house early next year, which is soon. It's going to be a big place with everything in it.

Shaz will live like a queen. She'll even have her own cleaner.

Anyway, Shaz just smiles. She's more Mother Earth and simple.

You know …

A honey-and-milk type of girl.

That's what Nan and Poppie used to call her.

She's goin' to the Goldie on the weekend. The community bus's goin' down. She likes bus trips.

Sue: How about hobbies? What do you like to do in your spare time?

Rob: Heaps, I …

        We like to go tarpin'.

Sue: I don't know what that is?

Rob: Well … it's this thing we do, like I'm sure others
        do it but we're probably the only ones doin' it
        here. Tarpin' all started from a dare, probably
        about two years ago. Dave used to do it when he
        was young. He says that tarpin' is an easy way
        for boys to prove themselves.

        Like, this is how real men play.

        Down the pub, they all know about Dave and
        how he went tarpin' when he was only fourteen.
        He travelled all the way to Caloundra on his first
        ride.

        His parents were pissed. They had to go down
        and pick him up.

        Didn't stop him, but.

        He's good like that, he's tough.

        We decided to give it a go, but no one wanted to
        go first except Pen. Which is stupid 'cause Pen
        was only thirteen at the time.

He's fifteen now.

Joey said he'd do it if we offered cash. Sixty bucks later, Joey climbed under the tarp of a Toyota Hilux parked outside the pub.

You've gotta do it by stealth or there's no fear and if there's no fear then there's no use doin' it.

We didn't know the owner but we knew he was local.

No, actually … Pen said the driver was a teacher at the Lutheran School. Pen said this guy's wife, who's real bonkable, is also a teacher.

She upped Pen once for a bit of graffiti on the back of the school library. Pen used to go to the Lutheran School before he got booted out.

Sue: So, you climb in under a random tarp without anyone knowing and you wait there until they stop driving?

Rob: Yep!

See, Joey had his phone, sweet as. When the Toyota Hilux stopped, he rung us and we picked him up.

It's an easy dare.

Sue: Does Shaz know?

Rob: Nah.

Miss, that's a dumbest question.

Why ya shaking your head?

Sue: I reckon things could go horribly wrong.

It's a stupid idea.

Rob: Yeah, well, like I said, that's the whole point.
Something could go wrong, that's the fear part
and that's why we do it.

Probably would be stupid if Sue was doin' it
'cause women are nothing but weak sooks.

Sue: What happened next?

Rob: Finally this teacher bloke comes out with a mate.
Both were wearing boardies, the passenger
wore a T-shirt and Vans, the teacher a shirt with
thongs. I remember the clothes because I had
the exact same T-shirt as the passenger and the

exact same boardies as the teacher.

Coincidence, eh?

Sue: True.

Rob: There was nothin' strange about 'em, as far as we could tell. They looked like mates goin' home to watch the footy, 'cause the footy was on.

Essendon vs Collingwood. It was a good game. The Bombers won.

Up the Bombers!

You know how I said it was an easy dare?

Sue: Yep.

Rob: Well, this was our first time. All of us were a bit freaked out. My guts churned around like somethin' bad was gonna happen.

Sue: Who's the sook now?

Rob: It was the first time, Miss.

Sue: Whatever.

Rob: I went through half a roll of those anti-acid lolly things so I wouldn't throw up or fart out a pebble turd or somethin'. 'Cause, really, when ya head starts thinkin', everything gets blown out of reality. These two blokes could've easily been serial terrorists or mafia gangsters or bikers undercover.

None of us knew them, not well enough to say g'day or how's it hangin'.

Yeah, things were a bit tense there for a while.

I was even thinkin' about what I'd say to Dave if Joey didn't turn up for work the next day.

Not even kiddin', the old man would totally throw a mental and then I'd be in the biggest, deepest shit.

Sue: What happened next?

Rob: Thankfully Foot received the call a bit after an hour later. The longest time ever, Miss.

Joey rang from the end of Buchanan Road, a mostly dirt track on the other side of town. Apparently the Hilux pulled up outside an old cabin backed up high in the bush there. Heaps of us know about it. It's dusty with cobwebs and huntsman spiders and probably pythons and browns. Nothin' much inside except a stone fireplace, a scratched-up wooden table and a few odd coloured chairs.

We used to camp out there when we was in Year Nine.

Just us blokes.

We'd say we were staying at each other's houses so parents didn't get suspicious. Joey just got his licence so he would drive us out with all our swags and food and grog and a few foils and bongs and stuff.

Sue: I'm listening.

Rob: I said we were taking drugs and you said nothin'.

Sue: It's your story.

Rob: So, as long as I don't say the F word …

Sue: Or the C word.

Rob: Come on, Miss? What's wrong with the C

word? Everyone says the C word.

The F and the C words are the most used words in the whole Aussie dictionary.

Every cunny funt knows that.

Miss?

Okay … okay.

If I don't say the F or C word I can say whatever I like?

Sue: Pretty much.

Rob: But it's my story.

Sue: It's your story.

Rob: You're full of shit, Miss, 'cause I should be able to say whatever I want.

Miss?

Okaya!

I get it.

Anyway, an hour or so after the Hilux drove off, Foot and me and Trev was driving Foot's old man's Patrol out to meet Joey.

Sue: So, Foot had his licence in Year Ten?

Rob: Na! Course not.

Sergeant Cole was out of town.

Anyone can drive if the copper's pissed off for the day.

Well, Joey wasn't himself when we found him, that's for sure. He was heaps away from the cabin. He must have bolted.

Joey was quiet.

Joey doesn't know quiet. If his mouth isn't movin' I bet you fifty bucks his arse is.

He's a smelly bastard, Miss. His farts could win wars.

After Joey calmed down enough to light a durry, he told us what happened.

Sue: Well, what happened?

Rob: Hold ya horses, I'm getting to it.

        It was big …

        And after he told us, we agreed …

        We all agreed dealing drugs isn't our thing.

        Long story short, that's how we found out
        Mr Lawrence, the deputy principal from the
        Lutheran School, had a little secret his loyal and
        very bonkable wife doesn't know about.

        Say something, Miss?

Sue: Maybe his wife's part of it.

Rob: No way, she's too uppity.

        Joey peeped through a crack in the boards. He
        said there was heaps of it on the table and on the
        floor.

Sue: Heaps of what?

Rob: Ice, Miss.

He upped it out of there real quick.

Sue: Did you tell anyone?

Rob: Dave …

He talked to Miss Piggy about it.

Sergeant Cole.

It was handled at a higher level, that's why it wasn't in the paper.

Sue: Sergeant Cole's a policewoman?

Rob: Nah, he's a he.

A bit gay, that's all.

Sue: Glad we cleared that up.

Rob: Not that it matters, Miss.

The whole man pluggin' another man thing doesn't worry me. As long as they don't plug me, all good.

Sue: Great to hear you're not homophobic.

Rob: Who's he? Nah, just kidding, of course I'm not.

Like, how long has it been?

Three

Four

Five years since gay marriage become legal.

It's law now so you just shut up and accept it.
That's what I do. As long as I keep me thoughts
to meself, I'll be fine.

Sue: What do you mean?

Rob: 'Cause, if Dave ever found out I was agreeing,
         I'd get a floggin' for sure. And so would Shaz
         probably, 'cause obviously those types of
         thoughts would come from her side of the
         family.

Sue: What's it like under the tarp?

Rob: If you can stretch out like I do, it's a sweet ride.
         When you're under there with a whole heap of
         tools and shit, well, then it's not fun.

         And that's when you wish you didn't beat the
         others to the dare.

Sue: What does it feel like after the trip, after you

make it back to your mates?

Rob: It's like Christmas when you were six or something. Not when Dave's home Christmas.

Christmas morning **without** Dave is the best time ever.

See, if you make it through to the end of the ride, the bigger the pay-off. You can actually make pretty good coin if you get a sweet ride. Fifty bucks to get under the tarp and a dollar for every kilometre you travel.

Everyone's expecting the big cash, like a trip to Brizzy or Byron or something, but we haven't cracked it yet. As soon as the ute stops at a servo or somethin', that's it, your trip's ended.

We never do it for nothin', there's gotta be a pay-off, 'cause why else would you do it?

When I'm underneath a tarp, layin' back and waitin' for 'em to stop, you'd think I'd be scared or freakin' out or goin' off me nut or somethin' but, nah, I just start thinkin' about shit.

If ya go tarpin' ya can't be a sook, sooks wouldn't last ten minutes under a strange person's tarp.

Only us blokes enjoy the buzz.

Sue: Did Pen have a go?

Rob: He used to, but … it's not his thing.

        Pen loves a joke and that but he's different. He's smaller than me and Joey.

        He's more of a big-thinker-type person.

Sue: I'm with Pen.

Rob: Thought so.

        Sooks stick together.

Sue: Aren't you scared?

Rob: Nah!

        Scared of nothing.

Spare Time

Monday, 2pm
Taralune High School, Library Room L2

Sue: Did you beep me at lunchtime?

Rob: Yeah! Me and Pen yelled out but you were too
        busy getting fuel.

        Did you see me new ute, Miss?

Sue: I saw a ute but I didn't know it was yours.

Rob: A Ford Falcon XR6 BA. It's exactly the same as
        Dave's.

Sue: Black with bars?

Rob: Sick, eh, Miss?

        Dave's present for finishing school.

Sue: But you haven't finished yet.

Rob: Close enough.

        Smoke 'em up, eh, Miss!

Sue: Young people and cars …

Rob: Chill, Miss. I'm a good driver.

       I'm gonna tell ya about Pen, Miss.

       Miss?

Sue: Okay.

Rob: Pen's small but he's the funny one. He knows
       lots of jokes and shit. And he's funny because of
       what he does … he cracks us up.

       Pen's work can be seen all over the district.

       He's famous online and everything.

       I'm not sayin' Pen's the next Banksy or anything
       'cause he's not.

Sue: So, he's a graffiti artist?

Rob: Yep and he's good.

       But the only thing he's good at painting is dicks
       and ballbags.

Miss?

Sue: I heard.

Rob: Well, say something.

Pen paints big dicks,

small dicks,

red dicks,

blue dicks,

green dicks.

He has to use a ladder for the big ones but the rest are easy. They can be found at the servo on Bells Road …

The big Shell in town …

Umm, let me think …

The school.

The community hall.

The back of the RSL.

All over the joint.

There was a really cool one on the back of the toilet block of the Catholic Church but this blackfella woman painted over it. It was huge.

Sue: The giraffe?

Rob: Yeah!

       You saw it?

Sue: Couldn't miss it.

Rob: It looked like a giraffe on steroids, pretty bloody funny, eh!

       Miss?

       Now every time Pen makes art, this blackfella …

       Lady …

       Comes along and paints over it.

       We didn't notice her here until about three months ago. Everyone reckons her work looks funnier than Pen's 'cause every animal she paints looks like a big dick with legs and a face.

Like, she's getting better, but …

Well, you know…

She needs more practice, eh, Miss?

Sue: Bless her cotton socks.

Rob: I don't know nothin' about blessin' people.

Shaz goes to church every time Dave pisses off, but … I don't know how church works. Do you, Miss?

I'll have to ask Shaz.

But it's not good for Pen when Shaz goes to church. Mrs Watson's there and she threw the biggest mental. Poor Shaz got a mouthful.

So, yeah … now the Catholic Church's a no-go zone.

Sue: But why doesn't Pen paint something …

More appealing?

Rob: Because.

Sue: Because why?

Rob: Because he doesn't wanna.

         And because adults don't like seeing big dicks
         and knobby nuts painted around town.

Sue: Ask a dumb question ...

Rob: What?

Sue: Nothin'.

Rob: Anyway ... there ya go, that's how Pen got his
         name.

         Pen is short for penis.

         Sounds stupid now I say it out loud ... he
         probably should be called Pee.

         Stop laughing, Miss.

         Shhhhhh! Everyone's lookin'.

Sue: What's your nickname?

Rob: Well ...

It was going to be 'stud' because of me killer blue eyes and awesome sixpack. But everyone thought I was up meself, so now it's just Rob.

Rob the heart-throb.

Sue: How about Foot?

Rob: Foot's got size seventeen feet or somethin'.

Sue: Thank God 'imself you got that right.

Rob: Yeah, eh?

Foot's always had big feet. His mum has to order his shoes in. I don't know when they'll stop growin', can't be too far away surely.

Foot's dad is another real prick. He comes and goes whenever he needs a good feed or a sleep or a roo ... I mean a fornication.

I reckon he gets plenty of everything wherever he is.

Him and Dave are mates.

Foot's dad never turns up to any of our footy games. He didn't even come to the awards night and his sons took out heaps of awards.

Dave went, and me and Joey got a trophy each. We were stoked.

But Dave wasn't.

We never heard the end of it. Apparently, we should've done better.

Always gotta do better.

Sue: What about Pen?

Rob: Pen doesn't play footy.

        I don't want to talk no more.

Sue: No worries.

        Draw or write, whatever you want. Use the tablet.

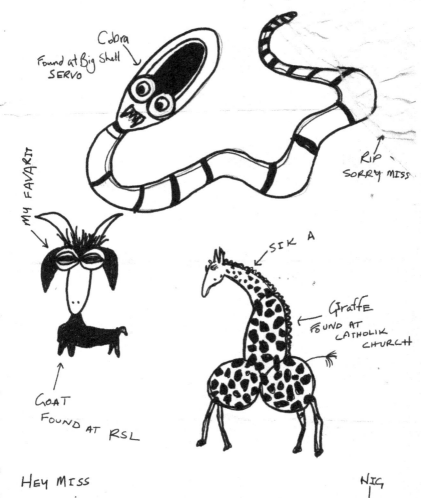

Nig

Sue: Tell me about this *mirrigan* of yours?

Rob: What's that?

Sue: Man's best friend, your dog.

        It's a Wiradjuri word.

Rob: Oh!

        Have you seen him?

        Nah, didn't think so.

        His name's Nig. He's the bestest dog. His coat is black and shiny as.

Sue: I figured he wasn't white.

Rob: Did ya?

        You must be psychic, Miss.

Anyway, he's a PB. A pedigree bitsa. A bit of this and a bit of that.

I'm not being unfair or anything … but Nig's the smartest dog I know. Me and Pen reckon he should be in the secret service or somethin'.

Pen and Shaz are the only people I trust to look after Nig. You know, if we dropped Nig off down where that new kid comes from, he'd find his way home again. Like, he's that smart.

I know you won't believe this but Shaz was cooking us dinner.

It was a stew and she left it on the stove.

Simmering …

While she went outside to take the clothes off the line, she sees our neighbour, Mad Molly, pickin' up sticks in her backyard. Shaz doesn't mind talkin' so she goes over for a yack.

Now get this … Nig notices somethin' not right with the stew and the stove. He barks but Shaz keeps yackin'. Shaz said she heard him but thought he was playing with somethin', a stick or ball, 'cause that's what he does sometimes.

Nig races across to Shaz and pulls her over to the house by her shirt.

Like, wow, what dog does that?

By the time Shaz is in the kitchen, the stew's boiled over, flames fired up by the gas were flickerin' and spittin' like that half-lady, half-snakehead thing.

Nig saved the stew ... he saved the pot. Maybe even the kitchen and when you think about it ... I reckon Nig saved the house.

Nig's a legend ...

Yep.

Sue: So, tell me ...

Who named him?

Rob: Nig?

I think I did ...

Nah!

It was ...

Dave.

Yep, it was Dave 'cause Shaz got me Nig for Christmas when I was still in primary school. Dave was away for ages, like two years, but he decided to come home for Christmas.

I don't remember much, but …

He said we were too old for presents.

Just as well Shaz got us some, eh?

He said the pup's name was Nigger. So, that's what we had to call him. It got shortened to Nig.

Shaz hates the name but she doesn't have a say, does she? Not when Dave's around anyway.

But it's a good name.

Don't ya think?

Miss?

Sue: Shaz isn't happy with the name.

Are you?

Rob: Well, yeah! Nig's my dog, Miss. 'Course I'm happy with it.

Sounds like you're not.

What's the big deal, Miss? Rappers in America use the word nigger all the time.

What do they call it ...

Re ...

It's um ...

Reclaimed.

They use it in their own way so now the meaning of it's all changed. It's heaps positive. Like, it doesn't sound so bad.

You even spell it different ...

N
I
G
G
A

It's not ... der ... og ... at ... ory anymore.

And don't forget most of those rappers are black, Miss.

So, it's okay.

Sue: Is that right?

Rob: Kin oath, Miss.

Sue: The word …

N
I
G
G
A

historically originated from the word …

N
I
G
G
E
R

Reclaimed or not, the word is connected to slavery. And slavery sucks. Black Americans were not the only black people enslaved in the world. Heaps of Blacks find the term offensive.

Rob: But Nig's my dog. I can call him whatever I
        want.

Sue: But you didn't, did ya?

        Dave did.

        He's a special dog, you told me that. If he's so
        smart and special, shouldn't his name reflect
        that?

Rob: You're giving me the shits, Miss.

        He's a black dog.

        That's why his name's Nig.

Sue: I'm a black person, right?

Rob: Yeah.

Sue: Well, I wasn't christened Gollywog, Suntan or
        Blackie?

Rob: You forgot Petrol Sniffer!

Sue: You cheeky little shit!

Kid in the Park

Tuesday, 11.30am
Taralune High School, Library Room L4

Sue: Hi, mate.

Rob: Can we start?

Sue: In a minute ...

Is this recording?

Rob: Don't press that ...

When this light's on it's recording, Miss.

Gee!

Sue: Thanks.

Rob: All you oldies are hopeless with technology.

Sue: Oi!

Rob: Well, it's true.

Sue: What do you want to say?

Rob: I had a nightmare thing last night.

        It kinda doesn't make sense.

Sue: You don't have to talk about it.

Rob: But it's my story so I can say whatever I like.

        It was about the old tree on Little Pomona Road.
        You know the main road coming into town?
        Well, there's an old tree there on the bend. It's a
        good spot for drifting. Locals call the tree Old
        Man.

        It's on the right.

        Probably …

        Ten …

        Twelve kilometres out of town.

Sue: I know the one, I stopped there for a look on the
        way in. I had to go back and touch it.

Rob: Yeah! Heaps do. The local Gubbi Gubbi,
        Trev's mob, say Old Man's special. He's a giant
        eucalypt.

A real good-looker and huge.

Anyway …

I don't know why but that tree was in my dream, nightmare thingy.

I wasn't doing anything.

And he wasn't doing anything.

He was just there right in front of me. Real close.

I could see every detail. Textures, colours. I could even smell the bark.

One night Pen was comin' home late from somewhere with Shaz and he said after they passed Old Man he looked in the side mirror and the whole tree was lit up from below. Like someone had a big spotty and shone it up through the ground, straight up the tree.

He told Shaz, but guess what? She didn't see a thing.

Heaps have got stories about Old Man. Some even reckon they've seen mass fireflies hanging around it. Like thousands of 'em. All tagging each other around the base.

I haven't.

I reckon they're full of shit.

Sue: Did Pen tell Shaz to stop for a better look?

Rob: You've got to be kidding. He wanted out of there.

They say it's sacred.

Sue: I reckon all trees are sacred.

Rob: Probably.

I've got to leave early, Miss, 'cause I've got kung-fu.

Sue: After school?

Rob: Yeah, but I have to do a few jobs at home first for Dave.

Sue: Got a note?

Rob: Don't need one, I'm nearly finished, remember?

I'm a senior.

Sue: So what?

Rob: So, I can come and go whenever I want.

Sue: Be buggered you will.

Rob: Come on, Miss?

Sue: Give me a note.

Rob: Dave will up ya if you don't let me go early.

Sue: No worries. I'll be here until four this afternoon.

Rob: God …

Sue: Apparently he's everywhere.

Rob: Hear that?

Sue: Thunder.

Rob: Come on, I need to help Dave before it starts rainin'.

       Miss?

Sue: There's not a cloud in the sky.

Rob: Did I tell you about the kid in the park?

Sue: Nah.

Rob: It happened a while ago.

       I was hanging around waiting for Pen.

       I hate waitin'.

       So, there was this kid sitting in the park
       opposite. He's in Pen's class. A few tools short.

       He's there all the time ...

       We call him Legless.

       He was drinking from one of those big Coke
       bottles.

       Anyway, he moaned. He fell off the seat, Miss.

Sue: Was he all right?

Rob: Yeah! He was pissed.

Sue: How do you know?

Rob: Me name's not Billy Hunt.

       Billy Hunt ...

As in …

Silly …

Sue: **Stop!**

I get it.

Rob: Anyway … like, we all know what's in the bottle …

Rum … scotch … vodka for sure.

He's a loser. He's always sitting in the same spot.

Soon as school finishes he goes straight there on his skateboard.

Why doesn't he go home?

Sue: Why didn't you ask him?

Rob: As if.

I went over and sussed him out. He hit his head and he had spit hanging from his lip. He was out of it. The dirty bastard even pissed himself. I could smell and see it.

Like, who pisses themselves in public?

Dirty bastard.

Anyway, I thought of taking a picture.

Sue:	Why?

Rob:	Post it online. He's a loser, Miss.

I left after that, Pen had to walk home by himself.

Sue:	What's your definition of loser?

Rob:	What?

Sue:	You heard.

Rob:	A loser is someone who does nothin'.

Drinks …

Does drugs …

Doesn't care about anyone.

What, Miss?

Work

Sue: What's happening?

Rob: Next week I'm working, no school.

Sue: Well, you'd be happy with that.

Rob: Rather be at school.

Sue: That's a turnaround.

Rob: I looked up the word nigger.

        I get what you're saying. But …

        Nig's twelve. He knows his name. I can't change it now.

Sue: Yeah, I thought about that.

Rob: And guess what?

        Trev's Aboriginal aunty hates the word blackfella. She says it's not a nice name.

        So, I was thinking … when you say the word

51

blackfella, it's the same as blacks in America using the name nigger.

Sue: I see your point.

Rob: You don't have a problem with the word blackfella?

Sue: Nope … but I do have a problem with the word blackie.

Rob: Why? They're almost the same.

Sue: I've heard the word blackie used disrespectfully.

Rob: They were being derogatory?

Do you know people who don't like the word blackfella?

Sue: Yep … and he's white.

I knew a guy nicknamed Nigger. He was always kind and generous, a real good bloke.

Rob: So, he's a blackfella?

Sue: Nah, white.

Rob: This is real confusing, Miss.

Sue: I agree.

For me, saying blackfella and whitefella is a simple way of stating the obvious. You're fair in skin colour and I'm darker.

Rob: So, it's about how it's said ...

Or how someone used it in the past.

Sue: Yep. Any word can be delivered with either vinegar or sugar.

Rob: But that's what I was saying, Miss. The word nigga is said with sugar.

Sue: Doesn't matter if you say

N
I
G
G
A

or

N
I
G
G

E

R

or

N

I

G

G

A

H!

The word has a history and its history isn't
sweet.

Rob: You know ... I thought Dave liked Nig.

Sue: I'm sure he does. He probably just picked the
name without thinking any different.

Rob: Nah.

It's because of Shaz.

Sue: What do you mean?

Rob: He calls her a Mussi.

A sand nigger.

Sue: She's Muslim?

Rob: Poppie's family were Afghani, they looked after the camels out west.

        But, nah! She's not Muslim.

Benny Boy

Name:	Benny Boy Conway
Age:	15
Year:	5
Pets:	Ramsi (dog)
	Narri (bird)
Nan:	Nan (Evelyn Agnes Draper)
Sister:	Mel (Mellisa Agnes Draper)

Benny Boy

Wednesday, 10am
St Nicholas Lutheran College, Taralune,
Room 5A

Sue: What's your name?

Benny: Benny Boy.

          Mum called me Benny.

Sue: Nice to meet you, Benny Boy, my name's Sue.

Benny: Yep.

Sue: So, what's your story, Benny Boy?

Benny: Dunno ... got no story.

Sue: Everyone's got a story.

          I was told you love fishing?

Benny: Love fish, love flatheads they're good fightin'
          fish and good to look at. Love snapper they're
          good to look at. But I don't catch 'em, only if I'm
          real hungry. I just like lookin' at them swimmin'
          and ...

I love cookin' and eatin' with my nan.

Sue: Is that who you live with?

Benny: I live with Nan.

          And Ramsi and … Narri Bird.

Sue: Who's Ramsi?

Benny: Our dog. He's got three legs and one and a half
          ears.

          And a crooked bark.

Sue: A crooked bark. What do you mean?

Benny: You know … like, he doesn't know if he's a pup
          or a grown-up dog. Nan says it's not strong or
          straight-up like a normal bark …

          It's crooked.

Sue: How about Narri Bird?

Benny: Narri Bird faints all the time.

          He'll be swingin' and talkin' up real neat one
          minute. Next, his toes are in the air.

Five minutes later ... he's back on the swing again.

He's narri.

Sue: He's got a few problems then. Poor old Narri Bird.

          Tell me about Nan.

Benny: She's pissed off. I ripped me new shirt for school, now she's got the you-know-whats.

Sue: What's she like? Is she funny?

Benny: She's fat.

Sue: You mean chubby?

Benny: Nah, she's fat.

Sue: Okay.

Benny: She's white.

          She tells deadly jokes. She learns me to read books and to be a good cook.

          She likes to sing with the radio. And ... she loves good manners, and Kylie Kwong's cookin' and hot chips with brown vinegar.

She don't like wearin' shoes … only when we go
shopping.

She fills me Coke bottle up with cordigal or
juice. I'm not allowed to have Coke. It rots ya
teeth and ya insides.

I like me insides.

And she has a beer every afternoon at
four-thirty.

Her nose holes always go wide when there's a
storm or new rain comin'. It's the brontide.

Sue: What is?

Benny: That thunder you hear miles away, that's the
       brontide.

Sue: I didn't know that.

Benny: And she likes smellin' the rain, says it clears the
       shite away.

Sue: Shite … ?

Benny: Yep. That's how me nan says it.

Sue: She sounds real cool, your nan.

Benny: Yep.

Sue: What do you like about living here, Benny?

Benny: Dunno.

I'm good at being friends, I like fish and drawin'
and feedin' the ducks. Better at drawin' than
talkin'.

Sue: Maybe you can draw your story? What do you
like drawing?

Benny: Fishes.

Sue: So, tell me ... who are your friends?

Benny: Well, there's ...

Pen with an N

Nan with an N

Narri Bird with a B

and ...

R
A
M
S
I

Ramsi.

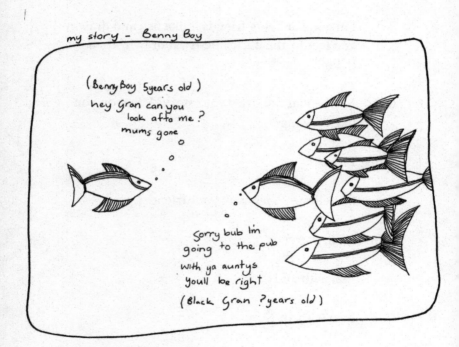

Foster Care

Wednesday, 12.15pm
St Nicholas Lutheran College, Taralune,
Room 5A

Sue: G'day, mate!

Benny: I'm goin' to see my sister this afternoon.

Sue: Cool! Is she close?

Benny: She's out Little Pomona Road.

         Every Wednesday, Nan and ... I, we, go to see
         her.

Sue: What's your sister's name?

Benny: Mel.

         She's beautiful.

         And kind and smart.

         Mr Malcolm and Clarice is next door. They're
         nice too.

I'm a foster bub.

Sue: I know a few foster bubs.

Benny: What are they like?

Sue: They're awesome just like you.

Benny: Are they happy?

Sue: Some of them.

Are you happy?

Benny: I love Nan.

She looks after me. Nan takes me out to Old Man tree in the summer when there's lots of storms around. Sometimes he's lookin' after all the fireflies.

Nan and … me have watched him babysit them all three times.

Sue: That's amazing.

Benny: There's thousands all around the tree.

I'm happy.

Is that all right?

Sue: What do you mean?

Benny: Nan's white?

Sue: Yep?

Benny: People said it's wrong.

Sue: Why?

Benny: They said I should live with a black foster nan.

Because I'm black. I'm Aboriginal.

Sue: Do you know anything about your biological family? Your blackfella family?

How about Mum or Dad?

Fear can force people to say many things.

Just remember ...

Love is ... more brilliant ...

And more powerful than the colour of our skin.

If your nan looks after you and loves you and you're happy to be with her ... that's all that matters.

Okay?

Benny: Yep.

Graffiti

Wednesday, 2.30pm
St Nicholas Lutheran College, Taralune,
Room 5A

Sue: Is this for me?

Benny: Look at it later. Okay?

Sue: No worries.

         Your head sore?

Benny: Yep.

Sue: Headache?

Benny: I'm all right.

         Did you see the giraffe?

Sue: He's solid, eh?

Benny: Probably needs a better neck.

Sue: Yep, he's definitely got a few issues.

         You know Pen, don't you?

Benny: Pen's my mate. He remembers my name.

His brothers call me Legless. Dumb name because I've got two legs.

Sue: Maybe they can't count.

Benny: Yeah!

The lady that paints on his work … she's funny. I like her a lot.

Pen's brothers go tarpin'.

Sue: Do you like tarpin'?

Benny: I love fishes.

Sue: Thank God for that.

Truth Be Told

Thursday, 9am
St Nicholas Lutheran College, Taralune,
Room 3B

Sue: Is this your note for the doctor's appointment?

Benny: Doctor Ross says I'm goin' good.

         No more attacks. Not since last year.

Sue: Seizures?

Benny: Yep.

Sue: You suffer from epilepsy?

Benny: That's how I got this scar. I fell off the bench in
         the park.

         Pen found me and got the ambulance.

         He visited me at the hospital. Him and Nan
         bought me hot chips with vinegar. We had a big
         feed.

Sue: How often do you go to the park?

Benny: Every day after school.

The Big Wait

Thursday, 11am
St Nicholas Lutheran College, Taralune,
Room 5A

Benny: It's my birthday today too.

Sue:　Well, happy birthday, mate. And many happy
returns for today.

Benny: Nan always says that.

I'm sixteen. I had my cake at breakfast.

Sue:　Nice one. Hope you made a wish.

Benny: Yep.

Got some for the park too.

Sue:　For this afternoon?

The park's beautiful, eh?

Benny:　Good place to wait.

Sue:　Who are you waiting for, Benny Boy?

Benny: Waitin' for Nessie.

Sue: Who's Nessie, your girlfriend?

Benny: Nessie's me mum.

        I've got no girlfriend.

        She went with Bruce in a Toyota Landcruiser.

Sue: Who's Bruce?

Benny: Her man. They're goin' round Australia then
        comin' back to pick me up and find a new house
        next to the river.

        Then I can watch the fish and I can feed the
        ducks and get me boat licence and I can look at
        the water whenever I want.

        Do you know Nessie?

Sue: Sorry, mate, I don't. But if I come across her I'll
        definitely tell her Benny Boy is well-mannered
        and an amazing storyteller.

Benny: Tell Nessie I sit in the park, at the bench.

        The one she said to be at.

Tell her I don't play with Thomas ...

Or Henry or Gordon ...

Or ... Percy no more.

And tell her I can touch the fan in Nan's kitchen now and I know me fishes ...

And ...

I want her ...

I would like her to come home now ...

Please.

Jack

Name:	Jack Trainer
Age:	17
Year:	12
Mum:	Mum (Coral)
Gran:	Gran (Lilly)

Jack

Jack: My name's Jack.

Sue: Pleased to meet you, Jack.

          So, you know how this works?

Jack: Yeah, I know.

          I don't swear too much around adults so don't
          worry I'm not like some others around here.

          Mum would crack it if she found out I said bad
          things.

Sue: I appreciate that.

          You right to start?

Jack: Just for the record, Sue, I don't like stories and I
          don't like writing stories. I'm not good at it.

Sue: See how you go. Telling and recording a story
          can be much easier than writing it down.

Jack: Still don't want to do it.

Okay …

First up, I know I talk like Mum and Nan. But that's the way I've been grown up. Everyone here says I'm old-fashioned but I don't care.

I'm from the bush, Sue; sometimes we talk different to the ones in the big towns and the cities. Ya see, I'm not urban like most of 'em here.

Sue?

Sue: Mate, I'm listening and I understand.

Jack: Ya do? Cool!

So, this is how it is. I'm not black. But my family are.

Sue: Great start.

Jack: Mum, Dad and Gran are all Koorie. They're part of a big Aboriginal family from down south. Gran is Dad's mum, she's been living with us since I was eight.

I'm seventeen now. Grandad's still kickin' but he doesn't live with us anymore.

That's a whole other yarn.

Sue: Sounds interesting.

Jack: Mum and Dad … I mean my blackfella Mum and Dad couldn't have kids, that's the first part. Second part is some white girl named Rayleen got pregnant with a white bloke from South Australia.

We don't know his name and neither does Rayleen.

Good on ya, Rayleen.

So, she had me on the fifth of February, that's my birthday.

Rayleen worked out she couldn't party much with me hanging off her hip or tit or wherever I was supposed to be hanging from, so she gave me away to her next-door neighbours.

Can you just give ya kid away?

You right, Sue?

Sue: Sorry, mate.

All good.

Jack: Well, the neighbours didn't have any kids, and, I'm not lying, they were on IVF. They were trying for a test-tube baby.

I know, who would have thought. Mum said I had beautiful milky skin, big green eyes and mousy brown hair.

Sue: And now you're blond.

Jack: Yeah, funny that, eh?

So … my new family couldn't wait to look after me proper.

Apparently Rayleen and I partied hard for the first few months.

Sue: Laugh out loud.

And the adoption's all legal?

Jack: Yep! Papers were signed and everything was made right.

All them do-gooders who think blackfullas aren't good enough to look after their own kids, well, there's their curve ball.

My blackfulla family had to look after us white kids too.

Eh, Sue?

Sue: Too right.

Jack: And they're the kindest … amazing … lovingest people I know.

        Is lovingest a word?

Sue: It is now.

Jack: You're funny.

Sue: Do you know what happened to Rayleen?

Jack: Yeah!

        Dear White Rayleen walked away and did the same thing, not once … not twice … but, wait for it …

        Three more times!

        Yep, I've got two half-brothers and a sister, and Rayleen didn't want any of us. Thankfully, fathers, other family members and neighbours came to the rescue.

No pity, we're all good, we're all better off.
Rayleen had the brainpower to hand us on. I
reckon she was good like that, eh!

Respect

Thursday, 1pm
Taralune High School, Library Room L1

Jack: I've been thinking about your T-shirt.

        'All Lives Matter'.

        Didn't think you'd wear that around.

Sue: Why?

Jack: Well, you're a blackfulla.

Sue: Yeah! And?

Jack: What about black lives?

        They matter too?

Sue: Absolutely …

Jack: So, you're a coconut?

Sue: Hello.

Jack: You are!

Sue: At least I've got some colour.

Jack: You know what I mean?

         Brown on the outside and white on the inside.
         You might look black but you think like a
         whitefella.

Sue: How does a whitefella think?

Jack: You know ... they don't care about blacks.

Sue: So, tell me ...

         What colour are you?

Jack: I told ya, I'm white.

Sue: Well, do you care about blacks?

Jack: That's stupid, course I do.

Sue: Well, what makes you think I don't?

         Just because I'm wearing an 'All Lives Matter'
         T-shirt?

Jack: I'm saying ... if you're one of the mob, you
         should be supporting 'Black Lives Matter'.

Sue: Mate, I may look black but I've also got Irish and
         Scottish blood running through these veins.

And God only knows what else is mixed in there.

I could be part Greek, Dutch, even German. The colour of your skin means little.

Jack: You don't care if someone calls you a coconut?

Sue: When I was younger, absolutely.

Not now … too old.

Seen too much and been hurt too much because of it.

I know me now. Saying someone is a coconut is hypocritical.

Jack: I just thought you'd care about your own people more.

Sue: I love people from all races.

Jack: But how about our Elders? They'd want you to support and respect black lives.

Sue: Elders or elderly?

Jack: There's no difference.

Sue: In my world there is.

The elderly live to an old age.

Elders are wise, profound, spiritual, strong, humble and have bucketloads of love for everyone.

I respect those who respect me.

Jack: So, you think you're an elder?

Sue: Me? No way, people give me the shits.

Jack: What people?

Sue: Teenage boys whose names start with J.

Jack: Well, who's the comedian?

Some elderly people are disrespectful?

Sue: Yep.

Jack: I know.

Gut Face ... our old next-door neighbour, she always had something not nice to say about my family. She was seventy-something.

Her head was big and round. It was real unnatural, like it was big enough for two people.

True.

If she was nicer I'm sure she would've looked heaps better but she was sour about Mum and Dad and Gran adopting me, ya see. She was always in a big old shitty mood, always.

Gut Face's kids … hadn't spoken to her in years. And she had seven of them. They didn't go near her even though they all lived in the same town. But I didn't blame 'em, 'cause I wouldn't visit her either.

I never called her Gut Face to her front, that wouldn't be right.

We were always respectful, even Mum, but I don't know why.

Funny thing was she cried on Mum's and Gran's shoulders when we left.

No one dogs on my mob.

Sue: Tell me about your family?

Jack: Well … everything was perfect … until Dad's
         heart broke.

         Dad was the type of guy who'd up ya for not
         looking after ya dog one minute and next he'd
         buy eighty dollars' worth of dog tucker and leave
         it in the back of ya ute.

         His heart attack was huge, apparently.

         Gran said that Dad was yarnin' up to Jesus long
         before his body hit the kitchen floor. And two
         hours later his blue heeler, George, keeled over
         dead on the front step as well.

         Dad left and George left and not long after hope
         pissed off and left us too.

         I can use pissed off, can't I?

Sue: Keep going.

Jack: We were shattered, busted up, and we was lost,
         Sue.

         It's the worst feeling ever. And after that, all we
         seemed to do was wait.

Gran, Mum and me were dog-tired of drownin'
in poor-bugger-me shit. Normally, it's not
welcome in our house, but somehow the bugger
found its way in.

Anyways … we wanted happy. We wanted to
listen to Billy Connolly and laugh till Mum
snorted. Mum's a big snorter.

We wanted to cross our eyes at Gran's funny
ways and go to the cemetery without snotting
up a bunch of Gran's homemade hankies.

It's all fine to want but how do you get your shit
together when hope does a runner?

I'll tell ya.

You can't and you don't. You just sit in your own
grey and darkness and wait for it to walk right
back through the door.

And that's what happened, Sue. Two months ago
we was living in our hometown, Tumbarumba,
close to the Snowy in New South Wales.

Sue: Tumba?

Jack: You know it?

Sue: I grew up not far from there.

Jack: Small world, eh, Sue?

Sue: Absolutely.

Jack: Gran was on the toilet. She'd been there for a while. Gran sings.

         Aha, she sings up whenever she's doin' a coonie. A big number two.

         Apparently piddling has absolutely no in-spir-at-ional value. But a decent-sized coonie is a goer.

         Gran's number twos always appear with a song. Always!

         Anyways, this day was different, Gran was singin' up real loud. None of the usual slow and morbid drawl she'd been singing since Dad and George left us. No way, she was uppin' Lady Gaga's 'The Edge of Glory' like she was singin' for the Pope or somethin'. She loves the Pope.

         Gran was back! Something happened, apart from the obvious, Sue. The toilet flushed and the door swung open and there stood Gran grinning real cheeky like. That's when I knew hope was back and standin' shoulder to shoulder with Gran at the toilet door.

I don't tell people I know many things, it's not part of my nature, but for sure I knew right then … at that exact moment, I knew my family was going to be all right.

And that was the night Gran was given a message. Move … Taralune.

How 'bout that, Sue?

Sue: Don't know what to say, mate.

Life's a mystery, eh?

Jack: Gran and Mum are great believers of talkin' to dead people and angels and that, so that's all we needed. Then and there, we made the decision. We rented out the house in Tumba, called the removalists. Had a party and a tidy-up. Picked up a couple of rocks from the garden then off we went to our new life.

Sue: Tell me about the rocks?

Jack: Gran and Mum have been doing the rock thing for years. Gran said her mum and her mum did it too.

It keeps your people, your country, with you.

See, and when you arrive at your new home, ya put the rocks near the front door or the front step, so there's a piece of your old life now part of the new.

Anyone can do it.

Aunty Leena, Mum's big sister, has moved so many times she pert near has her own pyramid sitting at her front steps. No wonder she doesn't have a bloke.

Why would you want to lug a heap of rocks around every time you moved? Movin's a good pain in the bum if you ask me. I won't be leaving here if I can help it. All that packin' and unpackin', I tell ya it's got big, fat, chunky knobs on it.

That's what I reckon, anyway.

Was that the bell?

Sue: Yep.

Jack: So, that's me, Sue ... Jack Trainer, adopted child
        of Coral and Keithy Trainer and twenty-first
        grandchild of Gran Trainer, now living on the

Sunshine Coast in a sleepy beachy town called Taralune.

Graffiti

Jack: Hurry up, Sue, I've got lots to say.

Sue: Go on then.

Jack: Oh, shit!

        Here comes stupid face.

Sue: G'day, mate.

Rob: Miss, this is the guy I was talkin' about.

Jack: Me name's Jack.

Rob: I know.

Sue: Don't you have some work to do, Rob?

Rob: Kin oath, Miss.

        Just thought I'd say g'day, that's all.

        G'day!

Jack: Ya numpty.

Sue: You've said it, now leave so Jack can continue with his story.

Rob: Is it as good as mine?

Jack: Better.

Sue: I've enjoyed both.

Rob: Yeah, well, I reckon mine's better.

Sue: See ya later, Rob.

Rob: Don't worry, Miss … I'm goin'.

Jack: Did you see what he did to my hair?

Sue: Rise above.

What do you want to talk about?

Jack: Well, you know the man body-part graffiti at the Catholic Church?

Sue: Yep.

Jack: Well, I helped Mum spray over it. Gran helps out too.

She holds the torch and looks out for anyone

coming. But Mum does all the creative work. She's only tall enough to reach the bottom half of the graffiti if it's big.

I do the rest.

Mum just tells me how to do it, you see. Mum and Gran can't work out why you'd want to spray-paint a male body part on a building. Mum says it's dumb and it gives her the dumb shits.

Whatever that means.

Sounds funny, but, eh? Dumb shits. Lol.

Anyway, the graffiti kid's name's Pen. I found that out last week.

I've met him … he's fifteen. Little fella, but funny as. So he spray-paints a male body part on a wall and then Mum comes along and changes it into an animal.

Mum loves animals and so does Gran. So do I.

Sue: You realise your mum, gran and yourself could also cop a fine if you're found out?

Jack: Yeah, we know, that's why Gran's always on

guard duty.

Mum says we're beautifying the town, you see. Her and Gran and me we also look after the cemetery and we're building a nice vegie garden all along our nature strip.

It's gonna be great when the vegies are ready to eat. And all the neighbours can have some too, you see.

Sue: So, you'll be a horticulturalist when you leave school?

Jack: Nah. I found an apprenticeship with a local builder, Dave Bower and Sons is their name.

Pen's Dave Bower's youngest son. Joey's the eldest and then there's stupid face, Rob. Rob and Joey are just like Dave.

Pen's nice like his mum.

Ya see, I must have presented myself pretty well 'cause Dave signed me up two days after I applied. I mean, I'm on probation for a month, just to see if I like it or not and if I'm good at it or not, and then, yep, I'll be an apprentice builder …

So, yeah.

Last week we did a job in the new housing estate, the Retreat. It sounds like an old people's home but it's for everyone who has money to spend and who wants to live on the rise close to the coast.

Gran and me think it's overrated. We could live in a shed somewhere and not be bothered much.

I guess the Retreat isn't for us mob.

Sue: So, how's it going, working for Dave?

Jack: I like the work ...

Sue: But?

Jack?

Jack: I like the work.

My dad was the best bloke. He was kind and understanding and he learnt me good.

Why can't other blokes be like my dad?

Sue: Everyone's dealing with their own battles, I

guess. Some deal with them well and others ...

Jack: Get angry and pissed off and rant and rave.

Sue: Do you need a minute?

Jack: Nah, I'm good.

Cemetery

Sue: What happened to you?

Jack: Nothin' …

        Got knocked with a bit of wood. I worked after
        school.

        Can we just start?

Sue: Sure.

Jack: Have you been to the cemetery?

Sue: Nah.

Jack: It's out on Little Pomona Road if you want to
        have a look. It isn't big, it's old but it's not big like
        say Wagga or Gympie. But that doesn't matter,
        it's in a pretty spot.

        The best spot in Taralune we all reckon.

        Mum and Gran are fatidous … fastid …

97

fastidious when it comes to cleaning and
weeding and sprucing resting places for dead
people. I'm probably just as bad.

We've only been here three months and Mum
and Gran just about knows everybody.

Mum and Gran are there twice a week, all day.
They pack smoko.

I used to help out every Thursday after school.

Each time they have a break they sit with
someone new. Last week it was Lilly Green who
died of old age and her husband Bob who died
three weeks later of a broken heart.

How sad is that?

The week before that was Rodney Blackney.
He's a 23-year-old local who drowned himself
in the river 'cause he was high on shit and was
drinking while trying to fish.

Sue: How about you?

Who did you have lunch with last time?

Jack: Let me see …

It was down the back and it was a black marble headstone. She was pretty with long brown hair and a cute dimple on her right cheek.

I remember because she had a clear photo. But I can't remember her name.

I'm not embarrassed I'm a bloke and I'm helping Mum and Gran clean up the place.

If Mum or Gran … or if I didn't live anymore I'd be happy if someone helped out and made things nice. I like knowing someone cares. I guess it's one of those things I inherited from Mum and Gran.

Eh, Sue?

Sue: You betcha.

Jack: Old Bill died from a shrapnel wound while fighting in Papua, he's next door to that girl whose name I can't remember.

          And Clarice has only a headstone, the rest of her grave is a big dip of dried dirt.

          Poor Clarice … I've still got to clean her up.

          Old Bill and Clarice are buried together but

they have different surnames. Someone said
they were girlfriend and boyfriend for years
but didn't get married. Clarice should be called
Clarice Malcolm same as Bill. I reckon they'd
both like that.

Mel … the girl I've been thinking about …

Her name's Mel. Mellisa Agnes Draper, 1980–
2015. She died when she was thirty-five.

I knew I'd remember.

Sue?

Sue: Benny Boy's beautiful smart sister.

Jack: Yeah! That's the kid who likes fish?

I know Benny Boy. Him and his nan keep Mel
looking special. We like Benny Boy and his nan.

Mel's always got fresh flowers and clean
water and a few candles too and she has my
favourite …

Six whirly windmills. They're real colourful like
a happy rainbow. Once the wind hits, they spin
fast as.

Sue: I thought all rainbows were happy?

Jack: Not all, Sue. Faded rainbows are tired. They give
        the people a show but, really, they just wanna
        chill and listen to Rodriguez or Paul Kelly or Cat
        Stevens.

        Happy rainbows are bright. And vibrant because
        they listen to AC/DC, you see.

        Anyway, whirly windmill things just like Mel's
        are awesome.

        You know the ones?

        We all like 'em, even Pen. Pen and Benny Boy
        and me and Nan reckon we don't want crosses
        on our grave when we kick it, too sad. We want
        heaps of whirly windmills.

        When Pen's hanging with Benny Boy out at the
        cemetery, he's the only one who has the patience
        to fix them if they come apart.

Sue: Whirly windmills make me smile.

        Especially if there's no wind …

Jack: I know!

That happens all the time.

Spooky ... but I like it.

On the other side of the cemetery fence the grass is knee-high, dry and full of seeds.

But ...

That's where I found five more graves ... they're just rocks, lots of rocks piled up on each other. Sharni didn't even know they were there.

Sue: Sharni?

Jack: She's a Murri girl. A Queensland blackfulla.

We both like movies. She doesn't care if I talk too much. She's a good mate.

I Dare You

Friday, 1pm
Taralune High School, Library Room L2

Jack: Gran can drive but when I got my L's I drove
        her around and built up me hours so I could get
        my opens. Now I have my P's, I'm still the taxi.
        I don't mind though, I like driving around, total
        freedom. I love it.

        Most of the time Gran's quiet but she likes
        AC/DC, we listen to it in the car all the time.

        She's the best gran ever. She doesn't even get the
        shits with grandad.

        That old bastard pissed off and left us, you see.
        Too busy chasin' some uppity old bitch with a
        pacemaker, perky titties and a bank account full
        of holidays and botox.

        And good riddance to the knobby-kneed
        bastard. Hope he gets piles on his piles and the
        mongrel has to eat soup for the rest of his life.

        I hate soup.

Sue: Say what you really think.

Jack: I did.

I just get frustrated. I don't get why he left us.

Not again …

Sue: What?

Jack: Here he comes.

Sue: Who?

Rob: G'day, Miss.

Sue: Rob!

Jack: Piss off, I'm trying to tell me story.

Rob: Calm down.

Sue: This isn't your class, Rob. You're in the next room.

Rob: Yeah! But I want to be in this one.

Jack: Ya can't.

Rob: Dave was right … you're nothin' but a sookie bogan.

Sue: Rob!

Rob: Come tarpin' sookie bogan. You might grow a
         couple while under the tarp.

Jack: Just like you didn't?

Sue: Enough, boys.

         Time to go, Rob.

Rob: Five o' clock Saturday, after the footy.

         We'll be in the park opposite the pub. Even if it's
         rainin'.

         Don't worry, Miss, I'm goin'.

Sue: Piles on piles, eh?

Jack: Yeah! Mum and Gran are going on the
         community bus early tomorrow for the
         weekend. They're going to the Goldie for a night
         out and lots of shopping. They're really looking
         forward to it.

         Those two'll run riot down there.

Sue: Are you going?

Jack: Nah! Benny Boy's going to show me his secret
        fishing spot down south head near Rocky Bay.

Sue: You okay?

Jack: Rob … the bloke's a flog.

        Just like his old man.

        The thing is, Sue … even if I was a bogan, so
        what? Being a bogan doesn't mean you don't
        have values or you're not loving or you don't
        keep the house clean.

        People've got that all wrong. Rob-the-knob's
        got it all wrong. The only reason he calls us
        bogans is because we're from the bush, we're a
        bit different and we don't have our own business
        like Dave.

        He's never met Mum or Gran and he's never
        been in our house, so why does he think we're
        not good enough?

        And I don't know why he's always talking
        himself up?

        His life isn't more valuable than mine … or
        yours or anyone's.

Sue: All lives matter?

Jack: I didn't mean it like that.

        But, yeah! I know what you're sayin'.

Sue: Tarpin's not for you.

        It's not for anyone.

Jack: I'm not scared.

Sue: I didn't say you were.

        I'm saying it's dangerous.

Jack: Don't worry, Sue ... I won't do anything stupid.

One person dead, two seriously injured in car accident

One male was killed and two males seriously injured when their Ford Falcon ute struck a tree near Taralune.

"Given the state of the vehicle, the impact was significant," said Sgt. Graham Cole. "Extraordinarily, the driver was coherent when help arrived. The deceased was found under the tarp. It's obvious speed and stupidity was, and continues to be, a factor."

Retired local paramedic Vince Reid was first on the scene.

The injured were airlifted to Brisbane. Names have been withheld until all family members are notified.

Tributes flow on social media as Taralune residents try to come to terms with the devastation.

The accident remains under investigation.

Lifeline Australia – 13 11 14

Queensland road toll stands at 200 compared to 198 this time last year.

Memorial Page
for 'Pen' Kane Richard Kateb Bower

Chrissie Lucas
This is the biggest waste. Pen was the best
person around. RIP Pen xxx
Don't know why you had to be like the rest of
them.

> **Birdie**
> But he wasn't like the rest of them,
> he had more brains and more heart
> and more funnies. I'm going to miss
> him heaps. Graffiti with the angels Pen
> xxxxxxxxx.

Trev
RIP Pen graffiti like you've never graffitied
before bro. You were the bestest friend anyone
could have.

Dodgy Roger
RIP m8, gonna miss ya jokes and ya art Lol.
Gonna miss ya.

Georgia
I can't believe you're gone Pen. RIP to the
funniest, loveliest, kindest person in the whole
school xxxx

Jack
You were always good to me Pen thanks. Mum & Gran & me will miss ya heaps.

Mr Potato Head
RIP kind sir.

Maryanne Watson
Words will never say what is needed here. You will be truly missed young man. May you graffiti with the angels. Condolences to your family.

Johno Johnson
RIP mate we'll all miss you. A quick recovery to both in hospital.

Tosser
Chrissie Lucas, he wasn't like the rest of them, that's why he did it.

The Butcher
If you're told all your life you can't do this and you can't do that, well eventually you want to prove them wrong. You never had to prove yourself Pen. Rest In Peace mate, in our eyes, you were always the bigger person.

Mia Rose

Poor Rob, thinking of you always
xxxxooo. Rest in peace Pen. You were
so awesome xx

Chrissie Lucas

Mia rose, get a grip you're not
even going out with Rob.

Mia Rose

Your just jelous Chrissie Lucas
so blow it out ya bum.

This comment has been deleted.

Leslie Peters

Grow up Mia Rose, this page is
for Pen.

Dreamgirl

Thanks for being so kind. Pen you were always
amazing. I'll miss you. xx

Grunge

What about Legless? I heard he pushed Pen
under the tarp before Rob got in the car.

The Butcher

You heard wrong mate. Get your facts
straight.

Grunge
I did old man.

Jack
The kids name is Benny Boy not Legless. It was Pen's fault he did it all himself. Benny Boy had a seezure 2 nights ago, the poor buggers been in the Noosa Hospital since L8 Fridy nite. he's coming home 2day.

Grunge
Where's ya loyalty Jack? You work for Dave so you should be thinkin of Pen.

Jack
I quit. And Pen was me m8 so pull ya scrawny head in Grunge.

Grunge
Jack; See You Next Tuesday.

Leslie Peters
This is really sad. Sorry to Pen's family.

Grommet
Thanks for being around Pen RIP.

Vince Reid

You young people never bloody listen, driving cars at high speeds can kill. Wake up! I'm sick of hearing and seeing teenagers in accidents.

This comment has been deleted

Mik

Grow a brain ya old faggot. We don't want to hear it. Think about the family.

This comment has been deleted.

This comment has been deleted.

Sarah

Yeah think about the family you idiot.

Andrew H

He's my cousin so shut up vince reid you old hairy arsed troll.

Vince Reid

The problem with you lot is you're not there to clean up the pieces. And if you did, you wouldn't be taking any more stupidity pills I promise that.

This comment has been deleted.

This comment has been deleted.

Johno Frazer
Well said Vince.

Kerrie McCabe
I agree Vincie

Leonie Talbott
Thoughts to the family, but yes Vincie you've hit the nail on the head.

Lionell singh
My sympathy's to the family. Vincie you said what we're all thinking.

Mia Rose
OMG Pen, I can't believe you're gone. Rest in piece wherever you are x

Carol Huchie
I never liked that tree.

Leslie Arthur
Nothing wrong with Old Man. RIP Pen, you were one in a million.

Johnnie
The tree's gotta go.

This comment has been deleted.

Will
Rest in Peace Pen.

> **Taralune Garden Club**
> Love, hugs and support to Shaz and
> family. We're here when you need us,
> Pen will be missed.

Lillie
Go fund me page is open guys, give if you can.

Steffie R
Why are we giving money? When my
family members die nobody asks for
donations … weird!

> **Nickers**
> Everybody's doing it now. End up dead,
> ask for money. I agree Steffie, this is
> weird.

This comment has been deleted.

Rosie
It's for his family you idiots, it's to help Shaz.

Harry James
True, Shaz won't get much help from Dave.
Rest in Peace Pen thinking of you little man.

This comment has been deleted.

Jacko McLean
His family's house's bigger than mine.

Carpet Snake
They've got a boat, I haven't got a boat.

This comment has been deleted.

This comment has been deleted.

Sally Anne
RIP Pen, will always think of you and your jokes
and your kindness xx

Neville Rowe
RIP old mate. How about a memorial at the
tree?

> **Grunge**
> I can get a cross made.

Andrew H

Yeah we need a cross and flowers at the tree.

Jack

Pen doesn't like crosses.

Grunge

As if youd no.

Bertha

No memorial near Old Man, just leave him be.

Lionel

I agree Bertha, that's what a cemetery's for.

Andrew H

Your right. Just cut the tree down.

Grunge

Good one Andrew H

Bertha

Why would you want a memorial at the place your loved one was killed at? It's a place of devastation and distruction and carnage. There's nothing nice about such a place.

Mr Bunnings
Maybe it's a reminder to go steady
Bertha. Just my 2 cents worth.

Chrissie Lucas
Only one person was holding the steering
wheel, can't believe Rob did that to his own
brother.

Carol Huchie
Chrissie Lucas it was an accident. Rob
didn't even know Pen was under the
tarp.

Sarah
It wasn't there fault. If anything it was
the tree's fault. They were going down
to Brizzy. Rob and Joey were just
clowning around like they always do.

The Butcher
They were trying to drift. That bend has
a reverse camber, perfect for drifting if
you get it right. Unfortunately the driver
buggered up. It won't be the first or the
last time it happens because you young
people continue to be dickheads and
push boundaries.

Carol Huchie
Thinking of you Dave, you're a great dad. One boy with the angels and one in hospital, hang in there love xx.

The Butcher
Great dad?

Carol Huchie
What does that mean?

The Butcher
It means he was a dealer. He may not have started it all but it didn't take him long to take over. How do you reckon he's paying for that big house out at The Retreat?

Andrew H
He's a successful builder.

Carol Huchie
Your wrong butcher.

The Butcher
Is that right Carol Huchie, loyalty goes a long way when you're a faithful customer.

This comment has been deleted.

Sally Ann

That's why there were heaps of cops searching Dave's sheds.

This comment has been deleted.

 Leslie

The first time we saw the fireflies last night, it was bigger than I could ever imagine. We're absolutely positive Pen was part of the magic. Rest in Peace mate xxxx

By Pen Bower
Year 10
Taralune High School

P.S. Hi Mrs Mac, there's lots of spelling
mistakes in the memorial page feed, but
that's how I wanted it. That's how we talk
and text and write. You said to be authentic
so tada!

Obviously this is fiction or I wouldn't be
here, ha ha. And anyway, if it turns out art
imitates life and I've got a couple of things
right, well, so be it I'm a genius! But, no,
don't worry, Mrs Mac, this is what I wanted
to write.

And thanks heaps for the introduction. Maya
Angelou is now my new favourite poet.

But still,
like air,

I'll rise.

Pen

Name:	Pen Kane Bower
Age:	15
Year:	10
Mum:	Shaz
Dad:	Dave
Brothers:	Rob
	Joey

Revelation

Pen: Keep recording, Mrs Mac.

Sue: But you've already written your story. I don't
       need to transcribe your work.

Pen: I just wanna talk things through. Gives me time
       to think.

Sue: Okay.

       But I'm driving home this afternoon, so this'll be
       a short session. I want to miss the storm.

Pen: It's been rumbling out there all week, nothin'
       will happen until tomorra, Mrs Mac.

       Trust me.

Sue: We'll see.

Pen: So, what ya think of me story?

Sue: Loved it.

       Confronting though.

Pen: Yeah. It was confronting for me too.

        It made me think about a lot of stuff.

Sue: Like what?

Pen: Like …

        Who really knows me?

Sue: Did anyone come close?

Pen: Jack did and the Butcher.

        He's an old family friend, the coolest bloke.

        And Jack, you know Jack.

        Benny Boy knows me but he wasn't in my story.
        He's not on social media.

Sue: Rob was driving the ute.

Pen: So?

Sue: That was powerful. Your brother was driving the
        car that killed you.

Pen: I had to write the Rob I know. It's something
        he'd do. Rob gets out of control. It doesn't mean

he doesn't have heart. He's got heaps.

People don't see it, that's all.

Sue: He loves Nig.

Pen: He loves all of us except Dave.

       We stick together, Joey, me, Shaz and Rob.

Sue: It's good to have support.

Pen: I know he's a pain in the arse and everything
       but …

       He looks after us when things get rough at
       home. If Dave's on a bender, Rob steps in every
       time. Dave's got no hope if Rob's there.

       You'd think Joey would step in, being the oldest
       but he doesn't. Dave's got Joey rattled.

Sue: Do you need to see someone? Talk things over?

Pen: A counsellor? Head doctor? Nah, school's
       already done that.

       We're good at looking after ourselves.

       What ya thinking, Mrs Mac?

Sue: Wasn't it hard, writing about your own death?

Pen: Dying's part of living.

Sue: True.

Pen: I'm not scared of dying …

Are you?

Sue: Nah. But I'm scared of leaving loved ones behind.

Pen: Yep, me too.

I don't reckon Rob's scared of dyin'.

Sue: You don't think so?

Pen: Nah.

Why would he go tarpin' all the time and be so out of control with stuff if he was scared?

Sue: In your story, you got under the tarp?

Pen: So?

Sue: So, why?

Pen: I'm not fearless like Rob.

         I wanted to know what it felt like to go all the
         way.

         Just wanted to do somethin' random and go for
         it.

Sue: And how did it feel?

Pen: Mrs Mac, it's a story. Just words on paper.

         I shouldn't 've done it. I shouldn't 've got under
         the tarp.

Sue: Why?

Pen: Because me dyin' would've broke Shaz's heart.

         Dyin' and leaving Shaz, my brothers and Nig
         behind is dumb and pointless. I'm still young,
         got things to do.

         And I think I'm bigger than that.

         I know right from wrong.

         You know ... I feel physically uncomfortable
         when I'm doing something I shouldn't. It's a
         warning. My body warns me.

I get why others do it. Why they keep pushing
and why they get themselves hurt or killed. They
don't listen.

Sue: To adults?

Pen: No.

They don't listen to themselves. Ya body feels
stuff. Even when I was writing that story, my
body was reacting to the trauma. I felt sick
writing about it. Even though I wasn't actually
there, I could feel it.

Sue: Deep!

Pen: I know. I only just worked it out.

Sue: Do you think we can stop others from tarpin'?

Pen: Nah, I don't think so.

I know Rob, he won't listen. They've gotta work
it out themselves.

Sue: You okay?

Pen: Yep.

Sue: So, what are you doing on the weekend?

Pen: Hangin' with Benny Boy and Jack. Rob and them'll be tarpin'. They're trying to make it to Brisbane. No one's made it that far yet ... not even Dave.

Might paint a few pictures ... beautify the town.

Sue: Yeah, was meaning to ask about that. Why not paint something more attractive and meaningful?

Pen: Mrs Mac, don't ya like me pictures?

Sue: They're colourful.

Pen: Which means you don't like 'em.

Sue: Which means there's lots of great things to paint and share with the world.

Yeah, you're right, I don't like 'em.

So, why do it?

Pen: Well, here's the answer.

I paint them because ... I can ...

And because it gives adults the shits ...

And because it makes people laugh.

Before Jack rolled into town I was getting' a bit bored with it but now it's the coolest thing ever.

Jack's mum and gran are the funniest graffiti artists I've ever come across. But, you know, they can't do it all on their own. They still need me.

Sue: Until you get caught.

Pen: I guess we're fearless in our own way.

Sue: Is there a difference between being fearless and being reckless?

Pen: Is there a difference between being fearless and proving a point?

Sue: Apart from giving adults the shits and making people laugh, your graffiti doesn't have a point.

Which makes me think you're only doing it for the likes.

Pen: Everyone wants to be liked.

The following Monday after returning home this email was in my inbox.

To: Taralune High School
From: Principal
Subject: Letter to the School Community

Dear Students, staff, friends and families of Taralune High,

It is with a heavy heart and great sadness that I write to inform you Jack Trainer, a Year Twelve student at the school, died on the weekend in a multiple vehicle accident, half an hour from Ballina.

Jack touched many hearts. He was popular, studious, helpful and creative. Jack always stuck up for the underdog. He had a huge heart of gold and a smile to match.

Jack's funeral will be held next Tuesday 7th March at St Mary's Catholic Church, Taralune, at 10am.

In lieu of flowers, donations may be made to the Heart Foundation.

This will be a very sad time for all of us who knew Jack.

Please keep his mum, Coral, and Nan, Lilly, in your thoughts.

Police confirm Jack's death was related to the irresponsible game of 'tarping'.

131

This school unquestionably disapproves of any such gamble with one's own life. In view of Jack's passing we hope tarping is now a thing of the past.

Vale Jack Trainer, you will be missed.

I would like to acknowledge Aunty Marg and Uncle Ron Herbert, Rose Allan, Sue Abbey, Marg Garraway, Deonie Fiford, Rachel Bin Salleh and my Magabala Books family. Your support and guidance has been immeasurable, thank you.

Sue McPherson is an award-winning storyteller who lives on the Sunshine Coast. Sue is an awesome mix of Wiradjuri, Torres Strait Islander and Irish. She grew up with her adopted family near Batlow in southern New South Wales. Inspired to write by her two teenage sons, Sue won the inaugural black&write! Indigenous Writing Fellowship from the State Library of Queensland (2011) for her manuscript, *Grace Beside Me*, which was published by Magabala Books (2012).

A regular writer for TV and film projects, Sue's 12-minute short drama *Nan and a Whole Lot of Trouble* premiered on ABC TV (2012). *Grace Beside Me* was commissioned by NITV (2017) to be its inaugural scripted live-action series, which debuted on Australian screens in early 2018.